WOMEN O
Modern Music
1999 EDITION

Project Manager: CAROL CUELLAR

TELL HIM

Words and Music by
LINDA THOMPSON, DAVID FOSTER
and WALTER AFANASIEFF

Slowly ♩ = 76

Verse:
Celine:

1. I'm scared, so a-fraid to show I care. Will__ he think me weak if I trem-ble when I speak?__

(with pedal)

simile

Tell Him - 6 - 1

4

D#m7   G#m7   D

hand.   But what you must un - der - stand,   you can't let the

A/C#   E

chance   to love him pass you   by._____

Chorus:
A   F#m7
Both:
Tell_____ him,   tell him_____ that the sun and moon rise

D6   Bm7(b5)/E   E   A

in his eyes.   Reach out to him___ and whis - per

Tell Him - 6 - 3

Verse 2:
(Barbra:)
Touch him with the gentleness you feel inside. *(C: I feel it.)*
Your love can't be denied.
The truth will set you free.
You'll have what's meant to be.
All in time, you'll see.
(Celine:)
I love him, *(B: Then show him.)*
Of that much I can be sure. *(B: Hold him close to you.)*
I don't think I could endure
If I let him walk away
When I have so much to say.
(To Chorus:)

ANGEL OF MINE

Words and Music by
RHETT LAWRENCE and TRAVON POTTS

Slowly ♩ = 96

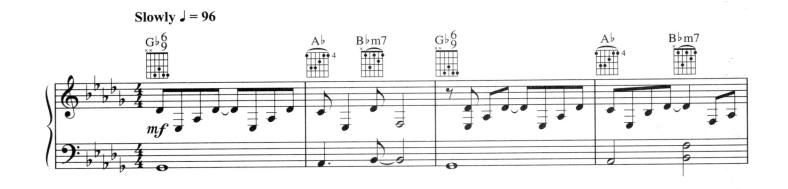

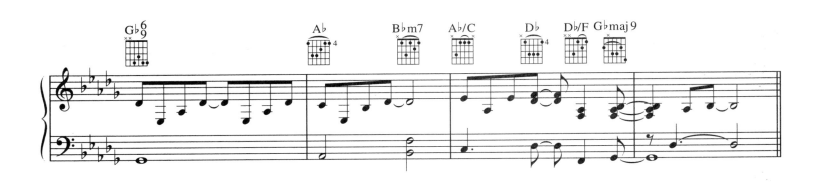

Verse 1:

1. When I first saw you, I al‑read‑y knew___ there was some‑thing

Angel of Mine - 6 - 1

10

12

Verse 5:

5. I look at you look-ing at me.___ Now I know why they say the best things___ are free._____ I'm check-ing for you, boy, you're right on time,___ an - gel of mine.___

rit.

HEAVEN'S WHAT I FEEL

Words and Music by
KIKE SANTANDER

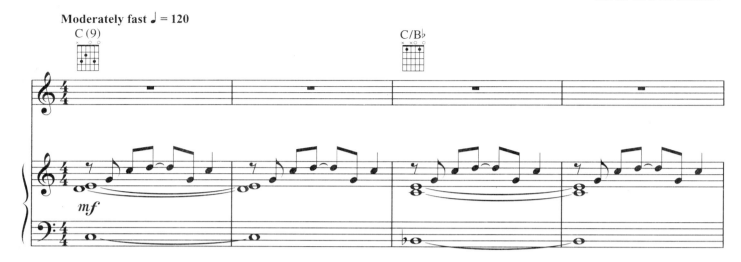

Heaven's What I Feel - 6 - 1

Pre-chorus:

Heaven's What I Feel - 6 - 6

...BABY ONE MORE TIME

Words and Music by
MAX MARTIN

24

CRUSH

Words and Music by
ANDY GOLDMARK, MARK MUELLER,
BERNY COSGROVE and KEVIN CLARK

Moderately ♩ = 100

Crush - 5 - 1

ANGEL STANDING BY

Words and Music by
JEWEL KILCHER

Tune guitar: D♭-A♭-D♭-F-A♭-D♭

Moderately slow ♩. = 66

Angel Standing By - 4 - 3

DON'T LET THIS MOMENT END

Words and Music by
GLORIA ESTEFAN, EMILIO ESTEFAN, JR.,
LAWRENCE P. DERMER and ROBERT D. BLADES

Don't Let This Moment End - 12 - 1

38

Don't Let This Moment End - 12 - 5

44

Don't Let This Moment End - 12 - 11

EVERY TIME

Words and Music by
JANET JACKSON, JAMES HARRIS III,
TERRY LEWIS and RENÉ ELIZONDO, JR.

Moderately slow ♩ = 96

Every Time - 5 - 1

*Fermata 2nd time only.

Every Time - 5 - 2

50

From This Moment On

Words and Music by
SHANIA TWAIN and R.J. LANGE

From This Moment On - 7 - 1

for better, for worse, I will love you with ev-'ry beat___ of my heart.___

1. From this

Slowly ♩ = 72
Verse 1:

mo-ment life has be-gun.___ From this mo-ment_____

you are the one.___ Right be-side___ you is where I be-long,___

HAVE YOU EVER

Words and Music by
DIANE WARREN

Slowly ♩ = 76

Chorus:

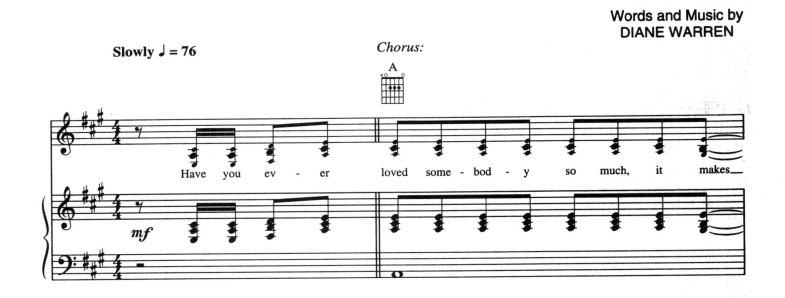

Have you ev- er loved some-bod- y so much, it makes___

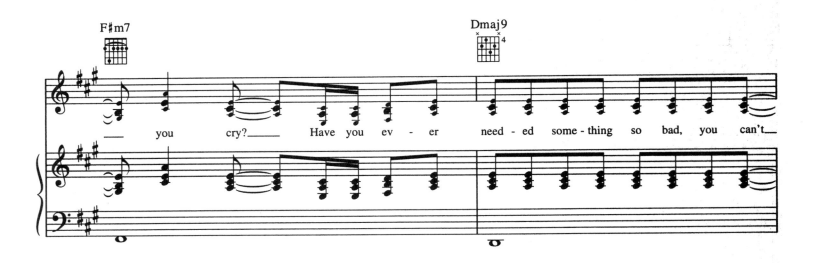

___ you cry?___ Have you ev- er need- ed some-thing so bad, you can't___

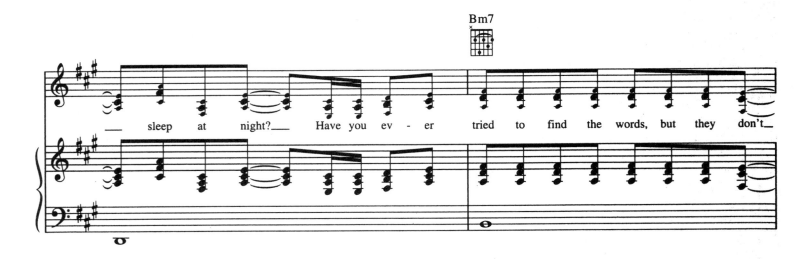

___ sleep at night?___ Have you ev- er tried to find the words, but they don't___

Have You Ever - 6 - 1

Have You Ever - 6 - 6

KISS THE RAIN

Words and Music by
ERIC BAZILIAN, DESMOND CHILD
and BILLIE MYERS

Kiss the Rain - 6 - 1

Kiss the rain.

Hel - lo? Can you hear me?

Can you hear me? Can you hear me?

Bass drum

Verse 2:
Hello? Do you miss me?
I hear you say you do,
But not the way I'm missing you.
What's new? How's the weather?
Is it stormy where you are?
You sound so close,
But it feels like you're so far.
Oh, would it mean anything
If you knew what I'm left imagining
In my mind, in my mind.
Would you go, would you go...
(To Chorus:)

FROZEN

Words and Music by
MADONNA CICCONE and
PATRICK LEONARD

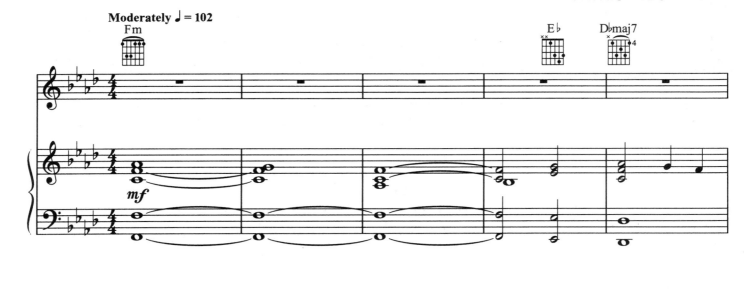

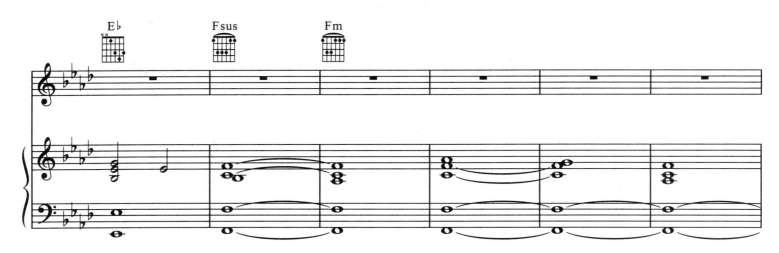

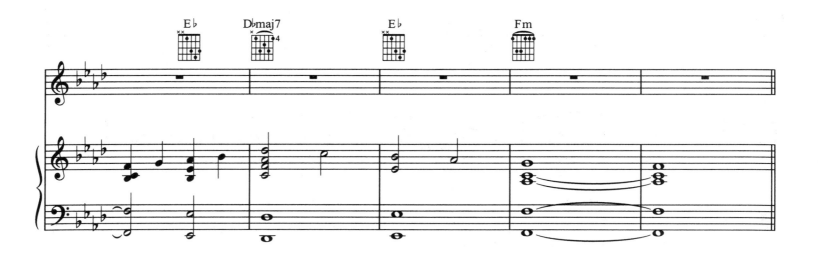

Frozen - 5 - 1

Frozen - 5 - 4

MY ONE TRUE FRIEND
(from "ONE TRUE THING")

Words and Music by
CAROLE BAYER SAGER, CAROLE KING
and DAVID FOSTER

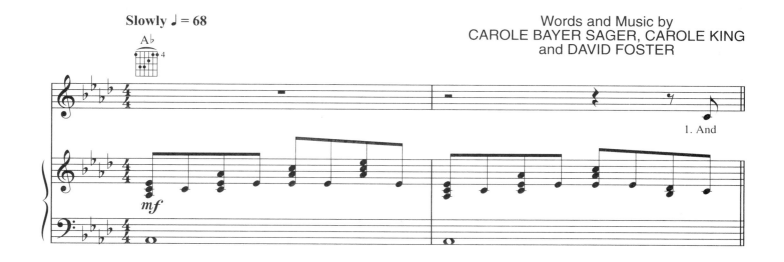

Slowly ♩ = 68

1. And

Verse:

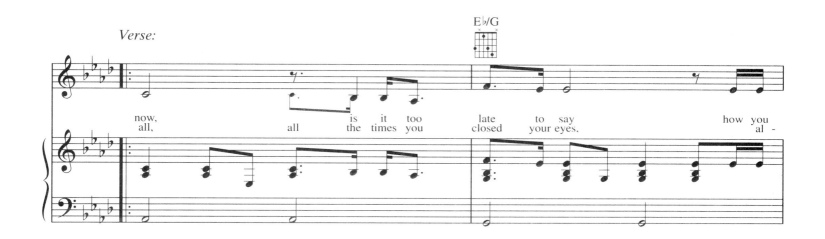

now, is it too late to say how you al-
all, all the times you closed your eyes,

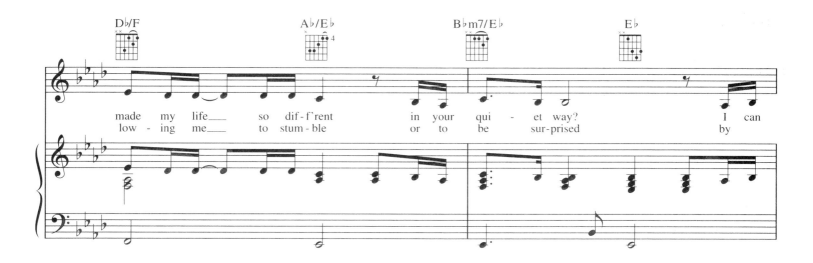

made my life___ so dif-f'rent in your qui - et way? I can
lov - ing me___ to stum - ble or to be sur-prised by

My One True Friend - 5 - 1

LET ME LET GO

Words and Music by
DENNIS MORGAN and
STEVE DIAMOND

Let Me Let Go - 6 - 1

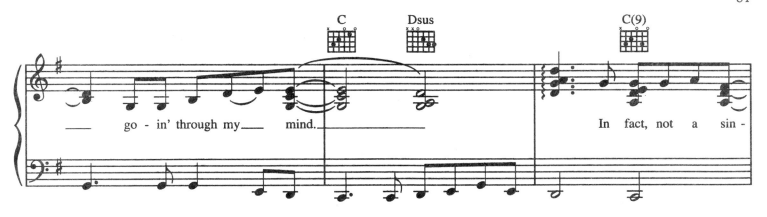

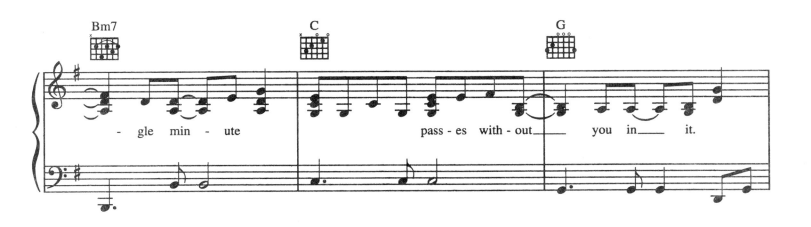

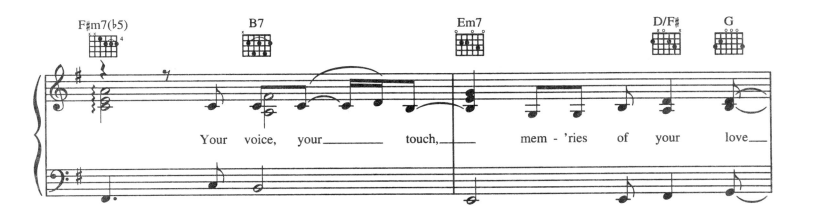

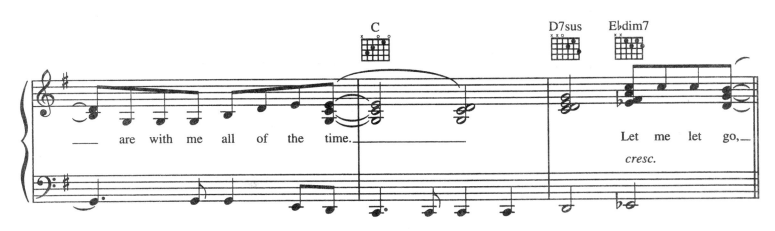

Let Me Let Go - 6 - 2

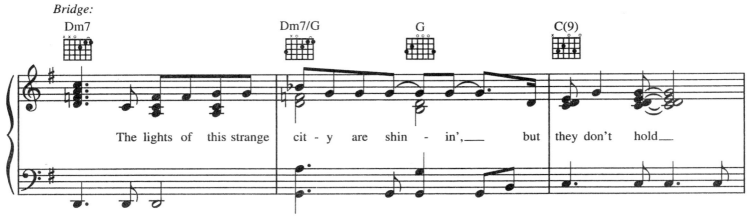

MY FAVORITE MISTAKE

Words and Music by
SHERYL CROW and JEFF TROTT

Moderately ♩ = 96

Verse:

1. I woke up and called__ this morn - ing; the tone of your voice__
2. Well, your friends act sor - ry for__ me; they watch you pre - tend__

__ was a warn - ing that you don't__ care__ for me__ an - y - more.
__ to a - dore__ me. But I'm no__ fool__ to this game.__

OH HOW THE YEARS GO BY

Words and Music by
WILL JENNINGS and SIMON CLIMIE

Oh How the Years Go By - 6 - 1

Verse:

94

And when the sun would_ shine,___ it was yours and mine, yours and mine for-

Chorus:

ev - er. And, oh, how the years go by.___

Oh, how the love brings tears___ to my eyes._ All through the chang - es the

soul_ nev-er dies.___ We fight,_ we laugh,_ we cry___ as the years___ go_

Verse 2:
There were times we stumbled,
They thought they had us down,
We came around.
How we rolled and rambled,
We got lost and we got found.
Now we're back on solid ground.
We took everything
All our times would bring
In this world of danger.
'Cause when your heart is strong,
You know you're not alone
In this world of strangers.
(To Chorus:)

RAY OF LIGHT

Words and Music by
MADONNA CICCONE, WILLIAM ORBIT,
CHRISTINE LEACH, CLIVE MULDOON and DAVE CURTIS

Ray of Light - 6 - 1

B♭ E♭ B♭ E♭ B♭ E♭
She's got her-self a u - ni - verse gone quick-
She's got her-self a lit - tle piece of heav-
ly, for the call of thun - der
en, wait - ing for the time when
threat - ens ev - 'ry one.
earth shall be as one.
And I feel
Chorus:
like I just got home, and I feel.
3rd time instrumental

And I feel___ like I just___ got home,_ and I feel._

To Coda ⊕ 1.

2.

Ray of Light - 6 - 3

NOTHIN ON ME

Words and Music by
SHAWN COLVIN and JOHN LEVENTHAL

Nothin on Me - 7 - 1

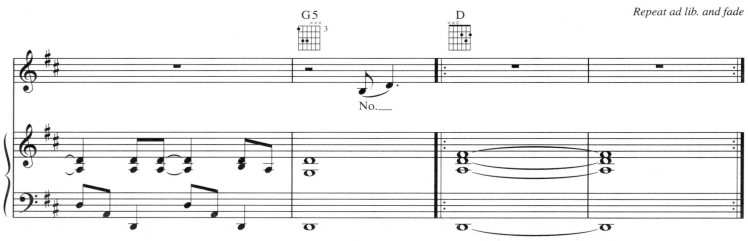

Bridge 2:
So, don't you try to save me
With your advice,
Or turn me into somebody else.
Cuz I'm not crazy and you're not nice.
Baby, keep it to yourself.
(To Chorus:)

THE POWER OF GOOD-BYE

Words and Music by
MADONNA CICCONE
and RICK NOWELS

The Power of Good-Bye - 7 - 1

112

113

The Power of Good-Bye - 7 - 3

114

The Power of Good-Bye - 7 - 4

116

The Power of Good-Bye - 7 - 6

Verse 3:
Your heart is not open, so I must go.
The spell has been broken, I loved you so.
You were my lesson I had to learn,
I was your fortress.

Chorus 2:
There's nothing left to lose.
There's no more heart to bruise.
There's no greater power than the power of good-bye.

STOP

Words and Music by
SPICE GIRLS, PAUL WILSON
and ANDY WATKINS

1. You just walk in, I make you smile. It's cool but you_
(Verse 2 see block lyric)

Stop - 6 - 1

122

Stop - 6 - 5

Verse 2:
Do do do do
Do do do do
Do do do do, always be together.
Ba da ba ba
Ba da ba ba
Ba da ba, stay that way forever.

And we know that you could go and find some other
Take or leave it 'cos we've always got each other
You know who you are and yes you're gonna break down
You've crossed the line so you're gonna have to turn around.

Don't you know *etc.*

HANDS

Words and Music by
JEWEL KILCHER and PATRICK LEONARD

Hands - 5 - 1

Hands - 5 - 3

Verse 2:
Poverty stole your golden shoes,
It didn't steal your laughter.
And heartache came to visit me,
But I knew it wasn't ever after.
We'll fight not out of spite,
For someone must stand up for what's right.
'Cause where there's a man who has no voice,
There ours shall go on singing.
(To Chorus:)

TOGETHER AGAIN

Words and Music by
JANET JACKSON, JAMES HARRIS III,
TERRY LEWIS and RENÉ ELIZONDO, JR.

Moderately fast ♩ = 120

Together Again - 7 - 1

130

THIS KISS

Words and Music by
ROBIN LERNER, ANNIE ROBOFF
and BETH NIELSEN CHAPMAN

This Kiss - 4 - 1

137

This Kiss - 4 - 2

139

This Kiss - 4 - 4

TOMORROW NEVER DIES

Words and Music by
SHERYL CROW and MITCHELL FROOM

142

B♭7   G7/B   G7(♯9)

pow - er___ of hav - ing___ you___ near.   Un - til___ that

%. *Chorus:*

Cm   Cm/E♭   Fm   G7(♯9)

day,_____   un - til___ the

Cm   Cm/B♭   Fm   G7(♯9)

world_____ goes a - way.   Un - til___ you

Fm/A♭   D♭/A♭   G7sus   G7

say_____ they'll be no more_ good - byes._____ I

Tomorrow Never Dies - 7 - 3

Un - til___ that

eyes._____

Verse 2:
Darling, you've won; it's no fun,
Martinis, girls and guns.
It's murder on our love affair,
But you bet your life, every night
While you're chasing the morning light,
You're not the only spy out there.
It's so deadly, my dear,
The power of wanting you near.
(To Chorus:)

YOU ARE MY HOME

Words and Music by
DIANE WARREN

Moderately slow ♩ = 84

Verse:

1. All of____ my life, I've____ been search-ing____ for some - one____ to find me.
2. You were____ the light in____ the win - dow____ when I could - n't find my way.

You Are My Home - 5 - 1

You Are My Home - 5 - 3

NO FOOL NO MORE

Words and Music by
DIANE WARREN

No Fool No More - 5 - 1

No Fool No More - 5 - 2

156

No Fool No More - 5 - 5